TREE *of* LEAF *and* FLAME

TALES FROM THE MABINOGI

DANIEL MORDEN
illustrated by BRETT BRECKON

Pont

To Bob Mole. Without whom . . .

Published in 2012 by Pont Books, an imprint of
Gomer Press, Llandysul, Ceredigion SA44 4JL

ISBN 978 1 84851 387 7
A CIP record for this title is available from the British Library.

© Copyright text: Daniel Morden, 2012
© Copyright illustrations: Brett Breckon, 2012

This book is published with the financial support of the
Welsh Books Council.

Printed and bound in Wales at
Gomer Press, Llandysul, Ceredigion

TREE of
LEAF and FLAME

Contents

THE FIRST BRANCH

Once there lived a king of Dyfed called Pwyll. He was courageous and clever and impulsive and impetuous.

Pwyll liked nothing better than adventure: whenever he could be, he was out hunting with his dogs.

On one occasion he was in a forest with his hounds when he saw a flash of red and brown between the trees. A stag! His heart quickened. He gave chase.

All day he pursued that stag. All day he came no closer. And a strange thing: the stag was silent. It moved as if it was from a dream: slowly, gracefully, as though dancing, while Pwyll's horse and hounds were stumbling, trampling through the bracken, streaming with sweat.

The forest became ever more dense, the way more difficult. The brambles scratched his face. The branches snagged his clothes. The longer the stag evaded him, the more determined Pwyll became.

Then, from nowhere, another pack of hounds set upon the stag. These dogs were like none he'd ever seen: fur as white as snow, ears as red as blood. They had the same effortless grace as the stag. Their jaws fastened on its legs, flanks, neck. Though he saw the dogs snarling and barking, though he saw the stag bellowing, the only sounds came from his own horse and his own hounds.

Pwyll pulled the strange white dogs from the stag so that his pack could feast upon its flesh.

Then the white dogs became still. They settled onto their haunches. They cowered from something above and behind Pwyll. His own pack whined, pulled back from their prize.

Pwyll turned.

A hooded grey rider on a dapple-grey horse watched him.

Pwyll said, 'Good day to you.'

The horse shifted. The rider on its back was silent and still.

Pwyll repeated, 'I said, good day.'

'I have no words to greet a man who pulls my pack off its rightful prize.'

Pwyll heard the voice not in his ears but in his head. 'I am sorry if I have offended you,' he said. 'My hounds have pursued this stag since first light.'

'The stag was mine. It was from my land, the land where I am king.'

Pwyll bowed. 'Again, I apologise, Your Highness. I am a king too. I am Pwyll, king of Dyfed. Please tell me your name and the name of your kingdom.'

'I am Arawn, king of the magic land of Annwn.'

'How can I mend my mistake? How can I win your friendship?'

'There is a way,' said Arawn. 'A nobleman wants my throne. His name is Hafgan. He is my perfect equal. We have fought since the beginning of time. I cannot defeat him, nor he defeat me. But if you became me for one year, if you took my likeness, wore my face, then when the time came to fight him, you could defeat him.'

This was meat and drink to Pwyll. To go to the wonderful land of Annwn, and to fight a creature from that land. 'I will! How do I find him?'

'A year from today you will meet him at a ford. Annwn is a magic land, and it has rules according to that magic. Strike him once and once only! He will fall, he will ask you to strike again, to finish him, but with every new blow you strike he will grow stronger.'

'But what of my land while I am away?' asked Pwyll. 'What of my people?'

'While you are me, I will be you.'

Arawn led Pwyll. When they reached the edge of the forest Arawn said, 'This is the border of my land. Goodbye.'

And he rode back the way they had come.

As soon as Pwyll moved beyond the trees it was as though he saw with new eyes. He looked at his hands. He didn't know them. He had never seen them before. He looked at his clothes. His brown tunic, his green cloak were grey now. His black horse was dapple-grey. His hounds were white with red ears.

Annwn! Never on a May morning had he seen a land so perfect. The colours were brighter, the shadows darker, the buildings finer than any he had ever dreamed of. Every passer-by greeted him as their king.

When he reached the hall of Arawn, the servants welcomed him warmly. From the way his servants spoke to him, Pwyll knew this Arawn was a kind and generous man. They helped him from his horse. They took it to the stables. They led away his hounds. They showed him to his bedchamber. Servants pulled off his boots and helped him out of his hunting clothes. They gave him bowls of warm

water. They washed him. They fetched him fine robes. They dressed him.

They led him to a hall.

A band of fine warriors entered. They bowed before their king. Servants fetched the best feast that ever Pwyll tasted.

As he ate and drank, a woman entered the hall. All the guests stood in silence, out of respect for her. The servants were still until she took her place at the table. Pwyll had seen wonderful sights in this land, but nothing had prepared him for the sight of this beautiful woman. She sat beside him. She put her hand on his knee. She kissed him. 'Ah, my dear Arawn, how was the hunt?'

Even Arawn's wife thought Pwyll was her husband!

All through the feast that evening, her eyes were on him. They talked and laughed. Her hand was on his knee. They drank from golden goblets. They danced together.

Pwyll began to feel uneasy. When the feast was over, Arawn's wife led him by the hand to their bedchamber . . .

She climbed into bed beside him. She reached out to kiss him.

*

The days became weeks.

   The weeks became months.

      The months a year.

Pwyll lived the life of Arawn. He was happy, hunting and dancing and feasting. The people of this land were wise and clever and just.

Every night he lay beside the king's wife.

All too soon, the day came. Everyone, noblemen, servants, farmhands, followed Pwyll to the ford. At the other side of the water a warrior sat on his horse, his sword in his hand. Hafgan. A giant of a man he was, broad and burly, dressed in white and red. An army of white and red warriors stood behind him.

He grinned. 'Do your worst!'

Pwyll and Hafgan charged at one another. With all the strength of his arm Pwyll struck. His sword shattered Hafgan's shield into shards and entered his enemy's neck, causing him to fall from his horse.

Hafgan lay in the ford, clutching his wound. The bright water became a dull red. He tried to stand but fell. He coughed. Blood spattered from his mouth and his nostrils. 'In the name of God, strike again. Kill me!'

'I will not,' said Pwyll.

Hafgan recoiled. 'You are not him! You are not Arawn! And yet you know my secret! What did I ever do to you that you should cause me such agony?'

Pwyll could say nothing. He had to turn away. He shouted to the enemy army, 'You! Who is the king of this land?'

The men on the other side of the ford replied, 'You are!'

Pwyll gave his sword to one of his men, climbed onto his horse, and rode to where he had first met Arawn. It was a strange sight, to see the mirror image of himself waiting for him, dressed in brown and green, astride a black horse. He said to Arawn, 'Return to your land, and you will see what I have done for you.'

As they passed each other, Pwyll became himself and Arawn became Arawn again.

Arawn returned to his land. He was pleased to see his servants and warriors, and his wife, after so long. But to them he had never been away.

That night, in the bedroom, he kissed his wife. She stared at him.

He said, 'What is the matter?'

'For the past year you have shown me only kindness, but you have not kissed me, you have not touched me. Why do you choose to do so tonight?'

Arawn laughed. 'What a friend I have in Pwyll! Because for the past year I have been away and another man took my place.'

When Pwyll returned to Dyfed he asked his people what kind of king he had been in the past year.

'My lord,' they said, 'never have you been so wise and generous.'

'For the past year I have been away. Arawn, lord of Annwn, has ruled over you.'

'Promise us, lord,' said his servants, 'that you will rule just as he did.'

In his bedchamber, Pwyll found a wonderful gift. A magic sack. No matter how much was placed inside it, there would always be room for more.

And from that day, Pwyll tried to rule as Arawn had done, wisely and well.

But still his heart longed for adventure . . .

*

A year later, Pwyll, in his hall, was restless again. Around him, his men feasted and laughed and drank and sang.

Pwyll stood. He lifted his hands. 'My friends,' he cried, 'the thread of days winds out without a knot or a twist! Not far from here there is a hill. The hill of Arberth. I've been told if a king or a prince stands on that hill, he will either be blessed or cursed. Today I will take my chances on that hill. Perhaps I'll return cursed. Perhaps I'll return blessed. Either way I will have a story to tell!'

His men cheered and raised their goblets to their brave king.

So Pwyll and his men travelled to the hill at Arberth. They saw it from some distance: rising out of a dense forest. They climbed to its summit. They heard birdsong, more beautiful than any they had ever heard before. The music was somehow both sad and glad.

A mist settled over the land. A white mare emerged from the forest. Riding the mare was a beautiful woman, dressed all in white. The only sound was the song of the birds.

When he looked at the woman, Pwyll was reminded of someone. But who?

'Go to her!' he ordered. 'Bring her here!'

They saw a wonder then. One of Pwyll's men rode down the hill to fetch her, but though her white mare was moving at a slow canter and his horse at a swift gallop, he could not catch up with her. The faster he went, the further she left him behind.

She vanished into the forest. The birdsong stopped.

When Pwyll and his men looked at the sky, the sun was setting. The day had passed as they watched the chase.

That night Pwyll could not sleep for thinking of this mystery, this strange woman.

Next morning he returned to the hill. Again he heard birdsong. Then came the wonderful white mare and the beautiful maiden on her back. This time the most skilful rider on the fastest stallion in Pwyll's court was sent to catch her.

The mare ambled along, while the stallion behind galloped as fast as it could.

At last, the rider returned to Pwyll. 'My lord, if I could not catch her, no one can.'

That night, again, Pwyll could not sleep for the thought of her. His body ached as though he had been punched and kicked. Was this a blessing or a curse? Perhaps he would spend the rest of his life tortured with longing for this woman he could not catch.

Early that morning as he dozed, he sat up suddenly. He knew why she seemed so familiar. She reminded him of the queen of Annwn. The wife of Arawn.

The next day,
    when he sat on the hill,
        when he heard birdsong,
            when he saw her on her horse,
                he was ready.

He galloped down to her and cried, 'Please, for the sake of the man you love the most, stop!'

She stopped. 'At last! It would have been better for your men and for your horses if you had spoken these words days ago. I come from the magic land of Annwn. My name is Rhiannon. Our king, Arawn, is married to my sister. She told me of your gentleness to her. I hoped you might help me. You killed Hafgan at the ford, but his brother, Gwawl the Bear, is just as cruel and vicious. He wants me for his wife. Unless I can find some other husband, I will be forced to marry him.'

'If you would marry me, Rhiannon, I would marry you.'

She seized his hands. 'You are reckless to say such a thing! Think of what I ask. Think before you speak.'

Pwyll swallowed. He still did not know what the hill had given him. A blessing or a curse?

He thought of the sleepless nights he'd spent thinking of her.

He thought of how bored he was at court.

He thought of his adventure in the land of Annwn.

'If you would have me for a husband,' he said, 'I would have you for a wife.'

'Then tonight, without delay, we must go to the palace of my father.'

And so once again Pwyll travelled to the strange land of Annwn. Rhiannon took him to the palace of her old father. A feast was held in his honour. Pwyll sat beside the woman he loved, dizzy with joy and wine. Never had he been so happy.

In the midst of the feast, a traveller, wrapped in a cloak, his head hidden by a hood, bowed before him. 'My lord, can I ask a favour of you?'

Pwyll cried, 'Anything!'

'Anything?'

'Anything! I swear!'

'Then I'll have her!' The traveller threw back his hood.

Pwyll saw a man as broad and burly and bear-like as Hafgan whom he had killed in the ford.

Rhiannon cried out in alarm. She dropped her cup. With her cry the hall went silent.

The man said, 'Every soul here in this hall heard you swear to grant me anything. I want her for my wife.'

'Why can you not think before you speak!' said

Rhiannon. 'This is the man I told you of. This is Gwawl the Bear!'

Then Pwyll turned to Gwawl. 'You have bettered me. She is yours. I will return to my land and never trouble you again.'

He bowed before Gwawl. He bowed before Rhiannon and her father. Rhiannon's eyes were filled with tears. Pwyll turned and strode from the hall.

*

The night before the wedding of Gwawl and Rhiannon, a feast was held in her father's hall. Gwawl and Rhiannon sat together, Gwawl laughing, jeering, leering. Rhiannon, beside him, was still and pale and gaunt.

A traveller wrapped in a cloak, his head hidden by a hood, bowed before Gwawl. 'My lord, can I ask a favour of you?'

Gwawl said carefully, 'That depends . . .'

'All I ask is that you fill my sack with food.'

Gwawl laughed and clapped his hands. 'Servants!'

Meat, bread, cake and wine were fetched, but no matter how much food was placed in the sack it always had room for more. Now roast chickens, lamb, boar, whole oxen were put inside.

Gwawl said, 'Will your sack ever be full?'

'Only,' said the beggar, 'when a man of great power steps into it and says, "Enough has been put inside."'

Gwawl grinned. He stepped into the sack. In that instant, the beggar pulled up the sides so that Gwawl was trapped within.

The beggar threw back his hood. It was Pwyll. He blew his horn.

His men, who had been hiding outside, rushed into the hall. They overpowered Gwawl's soldiers. They tied the sack tightly.

Pwyll bowed before Rhiannon. 'Before I speak, before I make another reckless mistake, tell me what I should do with him.'

'Gwawl,' said Rhiannon. 'Do you know the game Badger in the Bag? Promise you will not take revenge against us, and we will let you go free. If you cannot make us this promise, then you will be the badger. We will beat the sack with sticks until you are dead.'

'I promise!'

They untied the sack. Gwawl walked from the hall without a word. Before he left, he gave Pwyll a look hard enough to bruise.

The next day, just as had been planned, there was a wedding. Pwyll and Rhiannon returned to our world. They went to live in Dyfed.

*

For one year all was well. Every day the king and queen would go riding together in the beautiful land of Dyfed. So skilful a rider was the queen that she always left the king behind without effort. It was as though she spoke the language of the horses.

But sometimes Pwyll would see his people staring at her, glaring at her.

Then the noblemen of his court asked for a private meeting with Pwyll.

'My lord . . . that woman whom you brought from Annwn: she has not given you a child after all this time. For the sake of your country, for the sake of your people, take another wife.'

'I will not!'

'Your Highness, you must!'

'I am still king of this land. I am not yet an old man who must pass on his crown. In a year we will speak again.'

Another year passed.

'Take another wife. She is not one of us. Do we have to tell you what is said about the ways of the people of Annwn?'

'Gossip!' said Pwyll. 'Patience is bitter, but its fruit is sweet.'

During that third year Rhiannon became pregnant. She gave birth to a beautiful baby boy. But it was such a long and difficult birth that, after it, Rhiannon fell into a deep sleep. Six women were set to guard mother and child as they slept.

As the women watched, a strange sound filled the room. A strange sound and a strange scent. The oldest of the women fell asleep. The sound grew louder. The next woman's head fell forwards. The scent grew stronger. The next woman, and the next . . .

The women woke up at cockcrow. They had slept! They went straight to the bed. The mother was still asleep.

The baby had gone.

'What shall we do . . . ?' said the oldest woman. 'When the king and his nobles learn of this, we will be put to the sword.'

Another said, 'Listen to me. My dog has just given birth. I'll kill the pups. I'll cut them into pieces. I'll smear her with their blood. I'll scatter their flesh across the bed. We'll say she is a witch. We'll say she ate her child. It will be our word against hers.'

When the pups had been killed, when their blood had been smeared over the sheets, smeared over her face, when the hunks of flesh and bone had been scattered over the bed, the women screamed. Servants woke the king. He came running. Rhiannon was woken by the screaming . . . her face was sticky . . . she put her hand to her cheek . . . blood on her hands. Blood on the sheets!

'Where is my son?' demanded Pwyll.

One of the women said, 'The tales they tell are true. The women of Annwn are witches. She ate her child!'

Another said, 'She is as strong as a bear. She fought us all. I heard they eat their children in Annwn. Now I know it to be true.'

Another said, 'I saw it with my own eyes!'

When the noblemen heard what had happened, they said to Pwyll, 'The hill gave you a curse not a blessing. She is a curse on this land. Your Highness should have chosen one of his own for a wife. She has bewitched you. Her ways are not our ways. Now she will learn our ways.'

There was nothing Pwyll could do. His people had never trusted this strange queen from a strange world. Now they hated her for killing and eating their prince.

She was made to sit outside Pwyll's castle day after day. Her clothes became filthy, ripped and torn. Her hair matted into greasy clumps.

She had to speak her crime to every traveller. She had to carry those travellers on her back, as though she herself were a horse. But the burden she bore on her back was nothing compared to the burden she carried in her heart.

*

Now, far away, in the land of Gwent, there was another mystery. Every year, the horse of a nobleman became big with a foal in her belly. But no one ever saw the foals, because every year on May Eve they disappeared.

The owner of the mare was named Teyrnon. One year he decided to guard her throughout the night.

He lay in wait in the stable, his sword in his hand. The mare went into labour. She gave birth to a fine foal.

The mother was suddenly frantic with fear. She reared up. She rolled her eyes. She whinnied.

Teyrnon heard a dreadful sound.

Through the window came a great arm, shaggy as a bear. It lunged for the foal. Teyrnon struck it with his sword.

There was an awful scream and the arm lay severed and twitching on the ground. Teyrnon rushed outside. The beast was gone . . . but at his feet Teyrnon saw a wriggling bundle. He picked it up. He unwrapped it . . .

His wife was fast asleep in bed. He rushed to her and shook her shoulders. 'Look! Look what the night has brought us! Good has come from that evil thing . . .'

And he put into her arms a golden-haired baby boy.

They named him Pryderi. He made them so happy. Never was there such a child. His arrival had been wonderful and his childhood was wonderful too. Pryderi was quick and clever, strong and kind.

He grew so quickly! Before he'd even lived a year, he could run and climb and jump like a three-year-old.

By the time he was two, he was as strong as a six-year-old.

He was given the foal born on the night he was found. Soon he could ride better than many a grown man. It was as though he and his horse spoke the same language.

Then one day a travelling storyteller came to the court of Teyrnon. In those days, storytellers were always welcome, because they told magical tales of wonders and carried news from one court to another.

Teyrnon said, 'Where have you been?'

'My lord, I have been in the court of Pwyll, king of Dyfed.'

'How is my old friend? How is his wife, Rhiannon?'

The storyteller's face fell. 'Oh, my lord, have you not heard? His wife gave birth to a baby boy, but that same night her servants saw her eat it!'

Teyrnon's wife was appalled. 'How could any mother do such a thing?'

'She is a witch, from Annwn.'

Teyrnon's wife shook her head. 'What did the child look like?'

'They say he had golden hair. They say he was beautiful. They say he was as beautiful as your child, who sits before us here . . .'

Teyrnon's wife took her husband to one side. 'The servants are lying. Rhiannon did not eat her son. He was stolen.'

'How do you know?'

'Look at Pryderi! Look at his face! Do you not see the face of King Pwyll looking back? I know how it feels to lose a child. I could not live with myself if I kept the boy from his mother. I cannot let her believe she has killed her own son. I will not let her carry that burden.'

And so, even though it meant giving up the boy they loved so much, Teyrnon and his wife travelled with Pryderi to Dyfed, to the court of Pwyll. Outside, they saw a careworn, barefoot, grimy woman wrapped in rags, her hair matted into greasy clumps.

As they approached she stood and said, 'Can I tell you the terrible thing that I did?'

Teyrnon's wife replied, 'I know what you did.

You did no wrong. Your child still lives. And he is here.'

Rhiannon's grimy cheeks were wet with tears.

When Pwyll learned that his son still lived, and his wife was innocent, there was such rejoicing. That night the king and queen, who had been apart for so long, were reunited. Pwyll offered golden gifts to Teyrnon and his wife, but they would accept nothing. Rhiannon made the boy Pryderi swear that he would visit them whenever he could.

Like his father, Pryderi grew to be courageous and clever and impulsive and impetuous.

I wish I could tell you that their story ends here. But one day a message arrived from the High King of Britain, a message telling Pwyll to gather an army. War was coming . . .

THE SECOND BRANCH

Once, in a castle on the coast, there lived a remarkable family.

The oldest of them, the king of that part of Wales, was a giant called Brân, whose name means Raven.

His sister was beautiful Branwen.

Two brothers they had – twins. One was fair in looks and in nature. His name was Nisien. He always looked for peace. He could take the honey from a hive of bees without once being stung.

The other was dark in looks and nature. His name was Efnisien. He always looked for trouble. He could cause conflict between a cow and her calf.

One day, Brân and his brothers were out hunting. They came over the brow of a hill and saw a lake. They heard the silver song of birds. Ripples spread from the centre of the lake. Out from under the water rose a monstrous head, pale-skinned, fierce-faced, sharp-toothed, its red eyes blazing, its wild hair red as fire, long strong arms, hands like claws . . . A beast the like of which they had never seen.

Then another beast, a female, rose out of the water, carrying a carved cauldron.

Brân and his brothers drew their swords, but the dripping beasts bowed before them.

'Your Highness,' said the first creature, 'we are exiles from the land of Annwn. We would live in your land if you would allow us. In return we will give you two armies! An army of the living and an army of the dead. Every month my wife will give birth to two red-haired, red-eyed, fierce-faced warriors for you to command.'

'And this cauldron will give you a silent army,' said the monstrous woman. 'Put a dead man inside, and his eyes will open again. He will fight for you, without fear, without thought. He will obey your every instruction until he is hacked limb from limb. And the only way to destroy this cauldron is for a living man to climb into it.'

Brân turned to his brothers and whispered, 'Encounters with Annwn bring a blessing or a curse. Which is this?'

Wise Nisien said, 'Why do we need more warriors? We are at peace.'

Wilful Efnisien hissed, 'With them you will be feared throughout Britain. You will be High King of the whole of the Island of the Mighty!'

'We will have to feed them, clothe them.'

'No one will dare to challenge you. There would be peace throughout the land.'

There was Brân, in-between. He wished with all his heart that his sister Branwen was with them. The crown weighed heavily on his brow.

At last he said, 'I accept your offer.'

And so it was that Brân became king of the Island of the Mighty. His army of red-haired, red-eyed warriors was so feared, no one in the whole of Britain dared challenge him. The reign of Brân was a time of peace. The giant king was like a broad tree that offered shelter and safety for all who needed it.

Never did Brân use that strange cauldron. The thought of bringing the dead back to life filled him with disgust.

One day, he sat between his brothers on the walls of their castle at Harlech. As they looked out to sea, they saw a darkening on the horizon. Ships!

'Prepare for war,' said Efnisien. 'Summon your soldiers!'

'Wait!' said Nisien. 'Look! There, on the first ship, a warrior is holding his shield high. You see it flash in the sun? That means this fleet has come to speak with us, not fight.'

The fleet landed.

From the first ship stepped Matholwch, king of Ireland. He bowed before Brân.

'Your Highness, we across the sea have heard that you have mustered a great army. We have come to be assured that you mean us no harm, that you do not intend to invade us.'

'You are welcome here,' said Brân. 'I hope that during your stay I can make you understand that I mean only peace.'

That night a feast was held. Because of his size, Brân could not attend – no hall had ever been built that was big enough for him to enter. Instead Nisien presided over the gathering.

The Irish guests were wary, watchful. Nisien ordered that every Irishman be given a glittering goblet to drink from, a brilliant bowl to eat from and a warm cloak to wrap himself in. Despite Nisien's gentle words, despite his gifts, the Irish king, Matholwch, would return to the same question time and again: why would a king who wanted only peace gather such an army?

To this question Nisien had no answer.

Time passed and time passed. By day Brân would travel Wales, hunting with Matholwch. By night Nisien would entertain the Irish king in the great hall, with feasting and music.

Still there was doubt in the minds of the Irish, a lingering distrust. Nisien perceived one cause for hope. An affection was growing between his sister Branwen and the Irish king.

Nisien went to Brân. 'Perhaps, if all goes well between them, our two nations can find peace in a marriage?'

Brân went to his sister. 'Is it true what Nisien tells me? That you and Matholwch are in love?'

Her face fell. 'What if we are?'

'You have my blessing! I wish you happiness.'

Branwen wept for joy. 'Thank God! It feels to me that on this day my life begins.'

And so, with the wedding of the king of Ireland and the king of Britain's sister, peace was made between the two great countries.

Matholwch placed a crown upon Branwen's head.

A glittering brooch he clasped at her breast.

He wrapped her in a velvet cloak.

And a wonderful ring was slipped onto her finger.

I wish I could say that this is the end of our story. I wish I could say that Brân, Matholwch and Branwen lived happily until their deaths. But I cannot.

At the wedding, the whole hall drank and sang and danced and laughed together.

The whole hall? All but one. Wilful Efnisien.

Why was he the only one who could see the truth? His brothers were giving away the jewel of Britain, beautiful Branwen, to these strangers, these savages from across the sea!

This love-knot was twined too tight. Efnisien would have to cut it. He slipped out of the hall down to the stables. In the darkness, shifting in their stalls, were the fine horses of the Irish army. Efnisien went from stall to stall, slitting their eyelids to the bone, cutting their lips to their teeth.

The next morning, an Irish servant went down to the stables. He found flies and crows feasting on the flesh of the horses.

Brân was woken by a servant. The Irish fleet was setting sail! Brân, Nisien and Branwen rushed to the beach.

'What is the matter?' Brân asked Matholwch.

'Whilst I spoke an oath of love and devotion to your sister, you were cutting my horses! What kind of a people are you, who give with one hand and take with the other?' said Matholwch. 'I should have listened to my men. They told me you were not to be trusted.'

Servants were sent to the stables. They returned with the terrible news.

Brân said to Nisien, 'My brother, only your wise words can soothe Matholwch's wound. Do whatever you have to. Our sister's happiness, and peace between two nations, are in your hands.'

Nisien went to King Matholwch. 'This terrible act was done without the knowledge of our king. It was committed by my brother Efnisien. He can only see treachery! It is his affliction. We no more want war than you. War would mean women weeping on both sides of the sea.

'To compensate you, we will give a fine horse for every one that was maimed. Each man will be given a staff of silver as tall as himself, and a plate of red gold as broad as his face.'

But still the Irish were not content.

Nisien whispered to his men.

A carved cauldron was brought to the beach. 'Take it. Place a dead man inside and he will return to silent, obedient, mindless life.'

Matholwch bowed. 'This is proof of the truth of your words. If you wanted war, would you give us this weapon?'

The Irish furled their sails, anchored their ships and returned to Brân's castle. They stayed another night, then set sail for Ireland on the morning tide. Branwen sat beside her husband on a throne of gold and ivory.

Brân stood on the beach until the fleet reached the place where sea and sky met.

Nisien said, 'Your face is carved with care.'

'I fear for Branwen.'

'No man, woman or child can look upon our sister without loving her,' said Nisien.

Brân smiled. 'I wish I had your nature. You see only good in the world.'

Brân stayed on the beach alone, staring at the sea until the sky was bright with stars.

*

In Ireland Branwen was welcomed with great celebration. King Matholwch had found the most beautiful woman in the world for a wife! Every nobleman and noblewoman went to visit her. She gave them each a precious gift. For a year all went well. When a son, Gwern, was born, the whole of Ireland rejoiced. It seemed to Branwen that indeed her life had begun on the day she spoke to her brother of her love for Matholwch.

But during Branwen's second year as queen, Matholwch's closest friends, who had accompanied him on his voyage, went to him one by one.

'How can you forget what those savages did to our horses?'

'Your Highness, your people wonder why you allowed the British to commit such a crime without punishing them.'

'Your people say you married Branwen not out of love but out of fear. Out of fear of her brother Brân.'

The discontent grew and grew. One morning, as Branwen entered the great hall, she heard shouting. The entire court was gathered there. When they saw her they fell silent. They glared at her. For the first time she felt a foreigner in this land.

Servants surrounded her.

Her husband got to his feet. He went to her.

She said, 'What are you doing?'

He lifted the crown from her head.

He unclasped the brooch from her breast.

He took the cloak from her shoulders.

He pulled her wedding ring from her finger.

Just as she opened her mouth to speak, he struck her across the cheek with the palm of his hand.

The servants led her to the kitchens. She was made to sleep on a heap of straw. Each day she scrubbed the kitchen floor. Her white hands grew rough and raw. Her son, Gwern, was kept from her. Every morning the cook cut the meat and boxed her ears until her white face was stained with red blood.

All journeys to and from Wales were banned so that news of Branwen would not reach her brothers.

If ever she stopped to rest from her chores, a servant walloped her with a ladle. Her only friend was a starling who came to the kitchen window each morning. The servants laughed as she whispered to the bird and fed it the meagre scraps they gave her.

How they mocked her when one morning the bird did not appear.

Across the sea, Brân sat on the walls of his castle at Harlech. He heard a thrum in his ear, like the beat of a bird's wing. He heard a voice . . .

'Bran . . . wen . . .'

A note was found tied to the starling's foot. The note was read aloud. Brân threw back his head and gave such a shout of fury! The earth shook, the trees recoiled and throughout the Island of the Mighty flocks of birds soared into the sky. Messengers were sent the length of Britain. Every lord and prince and king was to gather an army.

In Ireland, a servant rushed to King Matholwch's hall. 'My lord, on the beach I saw a wonder!'

'What wonder?'

'A forest on the sea!'

Branwen was clearing the bowls and goblets from the tables. When she heard these words she stopped.

'A wonder indeed!' said King Matholwch.

'That is the least of the wonder. Behind the forest there was a mountain!'

Branwen turned her head.

King Matholwch was suddenly afraid. 'What kind of mountain?'

'Two lakes flickered and flashed on its high slope!'

Branwen laughed for the first time in three years.

King Matholwch said, 'My lady, can you help us solve this riddle?'

'It is too late to call me lady! That forest is the many masts of the British fleet. The mountain is my brother Brân wading through the ocean. The two lakes are his eyes flashing with fury at your treatment of me. Vengeance is coming.'

Such a battle then! Brân tore boulders from the rocky coast and hurled them at the castle walls. The sky went black with arrows from the battlements. The walls tumbled and crumbled to

rubble. King Matholwch and his men retreated across the wide river Shannon. They destroyed all the bridges that spanned it. Brân strode to the banks of the river and lay down so that his army could ride their horses over his back. Since then there has been a saying: 'He who is a leader must be a bridge.'

At this sight, King Matholwch was overcome with terror. He and his men hid in a forest.

The British surrounded it. At first light, they saw the forest had gone and a tremendous hall stood in its place, a hall big enough even for Brân to enter. Messengers were sent to him, inviting the British in, pleading for peace. Brân agreed a truce.

Wise Nisien said, 'I will go. This is our chance to avoid a tragedy. If the two armies meet in open battle, the only ones to gain will be the crows and rats and flies.'

'No,' said Efnisien. 'Let me go first.'

A vast hall rose high, high above Efnisien's head. The roof was supported by two hundred tree-trunk pillars. The king sat on a platform, surrounded by his court. In the centre of the hall was a fire pit.

Efnisien, eager to find offence, prowled the hall.

A peg had been fixed to each pillar, and hanging from each peg was a sack.

He grinned. 'Your Highness, what's in this sack?'

The king smiled back. 'Flour, friend.'

Efnisien put his hand inside. His fingers found the head of a man. Two hundred sacks – two hundred hidden warriors. Still smiling, Efnisien squeezed the head until the skull shattered. The king flinched. Efnisien pointed at another sack.

'And here?'

'Just flour.'

He reached inside. Crack! His spidery fingers crushed skull bone. Efnisien sneered, 'Flour? Flower! The flower of Irish manhood.'

Crack! Crack!

The king moaned.

When Efnisien at last emerged from the hall, he was wiping his hands. 'They are ready now, brother.'

Nisien went in. Two hundred sacks dripped from their pegs. The Irish king was trembling, his face pale as death. All the fight was gone from him.

King Matholwch agreed at once to Nisien's terms. For the sake of peace, the cruelty to Branwen, the maiming of the horses would be put behind them. The two nations would unite through Branwen's child. When he came of age, Gwern would inherit the thrones of both Britain and Ireland.

That night, the Irish held a feast to mark the

peace that had been agreed, and Branwen was reunited with her brothers.

I wish I could say that this is the end of our story. I wish I could say that Brân, Matholwch and Branwen lived happily until their deaths.

But I cannot.

At the feast, the whole hall drank and ate and spoke together.

The whole hall? All but one. Wilful Efnisien.

Why was he the only one who could see the truth? The Irish had won! This foreign child would one day take the throne of Britain.

Branwen said, 'My child, greet my brother Brân.'

So little Gwern ran to his giant uncle and greeted him.

'Now,' said Branwen, 'go to wise Nisien.'

And so Gwern ran to Nisien and embraced him.

Branwen fell silent.

'What about me?' said Efnisien. 'I would like to meet my nephew.'

Gwern looked at his mother. Branwen hesitated, then nodded.

Gwern, his arms outstretched, ran to Efnisien.

Efnisien threw him into the fire.

Such an uproar then! A cacophony of cries and shouts. Branwen lunged at the flames to retrieve her son, but she was too late to save him. Nisien pulled her back, for fear of the flames claiming her too.

In the midst of the chaos, Efnisien looked about. He watched the two nations brawling, the chaos, the tumult. And he smiled.

Brân put his hands against the walls and pushed. The high hall collapsed at his touch. Now the warriors fell upon one another. Everywhere there was the flash of blades and the crash of swords against shields.

A horde of hulking, fierce-faced, sharp-toothed, flame-haired, flame-eyed, white-skinned warriors fought for the British. The sight of the unearthly army made even battle-hardened Irish soldiers shake with terror. The British berserkers pushed the Irish back . . .

Then the men of both armies fell silent. The Irish army parted. Through the gap stumbled a dead man. He stood, swaying, silent, battered, bloody, a gaping gash in his chest. Another warrior, his head lolling, joined him. And another . . .

It was the Cauldron of Rebirth. The corpses climbed from the cauldron, incapable of pity or speech. Before long, the battle was between the two armies of Annwn, the army of the living and the army of the dead.

Unstoppable, the undead army hacked a path through the flame-haired horde, then into the British. Great Brân himself had to retreat, wounded by a poisoned spear.

Efnisien frowned. Everywhere he saw crows and rats and flies feasting on the flesh of the British. For the first time he knew the meaning of regret. The war he'd started would end not just with defeat, but with the death of Britain.

He crept onto the battlefield. He stripped an Irish corpse. He dressed himself in the blood-stained armour. He wriggled into a heap of the dead.

Irish soldiers came. They took the corpses to the cauldron and threw them in. Efnisien stretched his arms wide. With a terrible crack, the cauldron burst. Efnisien's heart burst also.

And so the battle was won by the British, but at a terrible cost. Only seven British warriors and Branwen were left alive. The flower of Irish manhood lay dead. Brân lay stretched out like some felled tree. He whispered to Nisien and Branwen, 'When I am gone, this is what you must do . . .'

By the morning the King of Britain lay lifeless. Nisien cut off his head. The survivors sailed to Anglesey and climbed a cliff. Branwen looked from

Ireland to Britain, each as desolate and empty as the other.

'I remember the day that I spoke to my brother of my love for Matholwch. The future seemed so full of hope; it felt as though my life was just beginning. Today my life ends.'

And there she died. You will find her grave on the island of Anglesey, on a cliff that overlooks the sea.

Nisien and his men travelled to London, where they buried Brân's head beneath the White Hill. Even now, ravens keep watch from the walls of the Tower.

THE THIRD BRANCH

Only seven Welsh soldiers survived. Only seven returned. Amongst the seven was Pwyll. In Ireland, he had fought and killed. He had seen sorrow heaped upon suffering. He had seen friends and comrades die. He surveyed the battlefield: too many corpses to count, too many to bury. As the rats scampered over the dead, as the sky darkened with flies, he swore to himself: 'I have seen enough blood for one lifetime. No more.'

Once the head of Brân was buried under the White Hill in London, Pwyll set off for his homeland. As he journeyed through the villages and towns of Wales, the sound of his horse's hooves summoned the people, eager for news of their loved ones. Time and again he had to speak the same awful words, to old men, women, even children. He remembered how long ago his wife Rhiannon had had to sit outside his castle, telling every passer-by that she'd murdered her own child, and he had some inkling as to how she felt. His heart was heavy at the thought of the loss of so many husbands, fathers, brothers and sons. He swore that he would do everything in his power to avoid such bloodshed again.

At last he arrived in Dyfed and was reunited with his wife and son. Rhiannon was overcome with relief that her husband had been one of the seven to return. Their son begged to be told tales of the Irish war. When he had been left behind Pryderi had been bitterly disappointed. He had been judged a year too young to fight.

Despite Pryderi's entreaties, his father would not speak of what he had seen . . . or what he had done. When Pwyll looked at Pryderi, it was as though he was looking into the past. He could see his younger self, impetuous and reckless.

Time passed without event. Pwyll ruled wisely over Dyfed.

One day, Pryderi burst into his father's court. 'Father, tell me of the hill at Arberth!'

Pwyll and Rhiannon exchanged a glance.

Pwyll said, 'Who has told you of this place?'

'I was out hunting. I met a traveller, wrapped in rags. I didn't see his face. He was more like a bear than a man! He said, "Why hasn't a fine prince like you climbed the hill at Arberth? Surely you aren't afraid?" What did he mean?'

'If a king or a prince climbs to the top of that hill, he will be blessed or cursed.'

'Have you been there?'

'I have.'

'And were you blessed or cursed?'

Pwyll smiled. 'Blessed! Because I climbed that hill I won your mother's hand.'

Pryderi cried, 'Then I'll go!'

'Think before you act,' said Rhiannon. 'The hill was kind to us. You might not be so lucky.'

'I was young,' said his father. 'I knew nothing of sorrow. Now, I would not go to that place. To see my wife and son each day is blessing enough.'

'You speak as if your life is over. Mine has just begun! If you climbed the hill when you were my age, why can't I?'

Pwyll could think of no answer.

'If you must go,' said Rhiannon, 'then we will go with you.'

The three of them travelled to Arberth. The hill was visible for miles around. It rose above the tops of the trees.

From its summit they looked out over Dyfed. They saw fields, farms, forests, smoke rising from homesteads, old men, women working, children playing, cattle, sheep grazing, cockerels strutting in the sunlight.

After a while they heard the silver song of birds. A twisting mist emerged from the forest. So beautiful was the song, they did not know if they listened for moments, hours, days or years.

The mist dissipated.

The people had gone. The homesteads still remained, but they were deserted. The old men, the women, the children, the cattle, the sheep, the chickens scratching had vanished with the mist.

All day, Pwyll, Rhiannon and Pryderi rode and saw not another soul. They returned to court, desolate, empty. The three of them were all that were left. In the whole of Wales they had only the birds and the wild beasts of the forest for company.

At first they lived on the stores of food at court. Then it ran out. They had to hunt, catch fish, plough and plant fields . . .

A dreadful loneliness settled over them. They became listless. An oppressive sorrow seeped into their bones, as black as the sloe. They would not speak for whole days at a time. They lost the will to forage for food.

Pwyll said, 'We must away to England. If we stay, we will die of grief in our beds.'

They rode to Hereford. For the first time in their lives, the king, queen, and prince of Dyfed had to work to earn a crust. They made saddles for horses. Rhiannon decorated them with blue enamel, adorned them with curling, swirling patterns. So beautiful were the saddles that soon the people of Hereford would buy no other. The saddlers of the city became jealous of these foreigners.

One day Rhiannon returned to their lodgings. 'Men in the street scowl at me. One of their wives whispered that they mean to kill us.'

Pryderi cried, 'They can try! The streets of Hereford will run red with blood.'

Pwyll said, 'I have seen enough blood. We will leave. We will find another city.'

They rode to Gloucester. They became shoemakers. Rhiannon decorated the shoes with golden buckles. So beautiful were they that the people of Gloucester would buy no other. Very soon the shoemakers of Gloucester became jealous of these interlopers.

Rhiannon returned to their lodgings one day. 'Men in the street scowl at me. One of their wives whispered that they mean to kill us.'

Pryderi cried, 'They can try! The streets of Gloucester will glisten with gore.'

Pwyll said, 'No. No more blood. We will move on.'

They rode to Ludlow. There they became shield makers. Using the skills she had learnt making saddles and shoes, Rhiannon decorated the shields with blue enamel and golden inlay. So beautiful were they that the people of Ludlow would buy no other. Very soon the shield makers of Ludlow became jealous of these outsiders.

Rhiannon returned to their lodgings one day. 'Men in the street scowl at me. One of their wives whispered that they mean to kill us.'

Pryderi cried, 'They can try! The streets of Ludlow will echo with the song of my sword.'

Pwyll said, 'No. We will return to Wales before another mother weeps.'

So they travelled back to Dyfed. They made camp, found firewood, ploughed fields, sowed seed, kept bees.

On the third May Eve after their return, they were hunting deer in the forest when their dogs started a white boar with red ears. Pryderi eagerly spurred his horse to chase it.

'Come back!' cried Pwyll.

Pryderi was riding the horse he had known since the day of his birth. The horse knew his every whim. As swift as thought they were, but somehow the boar was always ahead. It led Pryderi up a hill. On the summit he saw a fortress, a fortress he did not know. The boar ran inside. The dogs shrank back from that fortress, whining, whimpering. Without another thought Pryderi rushed in.

He found a marble courtyard. In the centre of the courtyard was a magnificent golden bowl, studded with jewels. It hung from golden chains that stretched into the sky above, as far as he could see. He grabbed the golden bowl. His hands stuck to the gold. His feet stuck to the floor. He could not move. He could not speak.

Rhiannon and her husband arrived at the fortress. They saw the cowering dogs. 'Pryderi!'

No answer.

She said, 'Surely this place comes from Annwn. I will go in and find him. If I do not return, swear you will not follow! Find some other way to free us.'

'I will go!'

'No, I know more of the ways of Annwn than you. Swear you will not follow!'

'I swear.'

She went in. There stood her son.

'What is the matter?'

He did not stir, nor did he answer. She grabbed

the golden bowl to wrench it from his grasp. Her hands stuck to the gold. Her feet stuck to the floor. She could not move. She could not speak.

Outside, Pwyll waited. Then he heard the silver song of birds. He saw a twisting mist emerging from the forest. The mist ascended the hill until Pwyll could no longer see the fortress.

The birdsong stopped. The mist lifted. The fortress had gone.

Pwyll would not leave. He paced and waited until the sky was bright with stars. He waited until day came again.

At last, racked with despair, he rode back to their camp.

Pwyll, alone, was like a man without a soul. His people, his family, everything had been taken from him. Days, months, seasons passed. He lived, slept, ate without pleasure.

The harvest was at hand. Three fields of wheat he had planted. When the first field was ready, he said to himself, 'I will reap it tomorrow.'

Next morning, a wonder! When he arrived at dawn with scythe and sickle, the ears of corn had gone. The stalks still grew, but all the heads had vanished. He shook his head in dismay.

'I will reap the second field tomorrow.'

Next morning it was the same with the second field. The head taken from every stalk.

The following night Pwyll kept guard over the third field.

When the field was silver with moonlight, there came a rustling sound. The ground around him began to seethe. Field mice, hundreds of field mice, streamed into the field, clambered up the corn and nibbled through the stalks just beneath the heads. Furious, he rushed among the mice to grab them. They were too quick for him. He lunged again and again and again. Then he saw a mouse that was slower, bigger than the others. He gathered it up and imprisoned it in his glove.

At first light he went again to the hill at Arberth. He set to work, with knife and sticks, making a little platform. A twisting mist emerged from the forest. He heard birdsong.

From the corner of his eye he saw a priest ascending the hill. Pwyll continued his task.

'Good day!' said the priest.

'And to you. What brings you here? I have not seen another man for three years.'

The priest shifted from foot to foot. He huffed and spluttered. 'I'm . . . passing through. I've just come from England. Tell me, what are you doing there, with sticks and knife?'

'Making a scaffold.'

'A scaffold?' said the priest, appalled. 'Why?'

'I caught one of the thieves who stole my corn. I mean to hang it.'

'What kind of thief can you hang from such a tiny scaffold?'

'Why do you ask?'

'I have here two golden coins. I'll give you them in exchange for your thief . . . whoever or whatever it might be!'

'I'd rather have two treasures. My wife and son.'

'What do I know of your wife and son?'

The priest turned and descended the hill.

The little platform was finished. So, with his knife, Pwyll began carving a gallows pole.

'Good day!'

Pwyll looked up from his work. There before him stood a man dressed as a Welsh noble. The man was sweating, anxious.

'Good day,' said Pwyll. 'Tell me, my lord, where have you come from?'

'Oh . . .' said the lord, and gestured vaguely. 'What have you there in the glove?'

'A mouse.'

'A mouse? You mean to hang a mouse?'

'How do you know I mean to hang him?'

'Well,' said the lord, 'because of the scaffold there. But surely you can see that what you mean to do is madness! Let it be. Here, I have a bag filled with treasure – gold, silver, jewels. I'll give you them all for the mouse.'

'No gold is worth as much to me as my wife Rhiannon.

'No silver as much as my son Pryderi.

'No jewels as much as the people of this land.

'Give me them, and I will give you this mouse.'

'How can I give you what is not in my power to give?'

Pwyll resumed his work.

The lord descended the hill and disappeared into the woods.

Now Pwyll unthreaded the thong from his boot and fixed it to the gallows pole. He took the mouse from his glove . . .

'Good day!'

He looked up. There stood a man dressed as a king.

Pwyll said nothing. He twisted the thong around the mouse's neck.

'I will give you a sack of gold in exchange for that mouse!'

'You know my terms.'

'What do you mean? We have just met!'

The mouse wriggled in Pwyll's hand. He tied the noose into a knot.

Urgently, the king reached for the mouse . . . 'A sack of gold and a sack of silver for her!'

'Her? Who is she then, and who are you?'

'A sack of gold, a sack of silver and a sack of jewels!'

'My wife, my son and my people. And tell me who you are.'

The king seemed to flicker and melt. In his place, there stood Pwyll's old enemy.

'Gwawl the Bear! You are the one who made all of this misery.'

'No, it was you. You brought this misery on yourself! You killed my brother Hafgan at the ford. You trapped me in that bag. You made me look a fool before my whole court!

'So with my magic I stole the people from Wales.

'I stole your wife and son.

'My men and I became mice and took your corn.

'On the third night of theft, my wife came with us. She was too slow. She is heavy with my child, so you caught her. Please, let her go!'

'For the sake of the love you feel for wife and child, give me back mine.'

'You shall have them!'

'Return the people of Wales to their homes.'

'I will!'

'And swear you will never again use your magic against my family or my people.'

Gwawl's face twisted into a snarl. 'I swear. It was as well you made me. Now, give me my wife!'

'Not until you undo the wrong you have done.'

'Look!'

The mist dissipated. Pwyll looked out over Dyfed. He saw fields, farms, forests, smoke rising from homesteads, old men, women working, children playing, cattle, sheep grazing, cockerels strutting in the sunlight. And Pwyll saw Rhiannon and Pryderi ascending the hill.

'Now, give me my wife!'

Pwyll gently placed the mouse on the ground. It flickered, and then in its place there stood a beautiful young woman, heavy with a child in her belly. She and Gwawl fell into one another's arms.

Gwawl was true to his word. Never again did he attack Pwyll's kingdom.

And so at last, Pwyll, Rhiannon and Pryderi lived untroubled by the trials of Annwn.

Never again did mist enshroud Dyfed's hills and valleys and never again did mice strip bare its fields of waving wheat.

THE FOURTH BRANCH

In north Wales lived two tremendous magicians, a husband and wife.

As Gwydion and Arianrhod grew in power, their love was soured by rivalry and jealousy, until they could no longer live together.

Gwydion built Caer Dathyl, a fortress on top of a mountain.

Arianrhod conjured a glass castle out to sea. Caer Arianrhod. At night, travellers glimpsed it glittering and mistook it for a constellation of stars.

Gwydion invited his estranged wife to a contest of magic.

Although she knew Gwydion was planning some elaborate humiliation for her, her pride would not allow her to refuse.

As Arianrhod entered his hall, she saw him brandishing a wand. He held it out. 'You are my wife. You always will be. And here is proof. Step over this.'

Before the court, she had no choice. She stepped over the wand . . .

From beneath her skirts dropped two strange 'somethings', stunted, half-formed boy children. One of them fled to the sea, where he became Dylan Eil Ton, King of the Tumbling Waves. Gwydion grabbed the other child. He laid the squirming thing in a chest at the foot of his bed.

He was woken one morning by crying. He took the child to a woman who was suckling a baby of her own. He paid her to suckle the strange boy as well.

At the end of one year the boy was walking and talking. At the end of two he was a strapping lad. At the age of three he was a handsome young man, who could ride a horse and loose an arrow from a bow with deadly accuracy.

Gwydion took the boy by boat to the glittering palace of Arianrhod.

'Why have you come here? And who is this?'

'Can't you tell? It is your son.'

'First you humiliate me in your court; now you try to do the same in mine! What is his name?'

'He has none as yet.'

'Well then, I swear this fate upon him . . . He shall have no name until I give it to him.'

Gwydion left Caer Arianrhod with his son, waited a month, then went to a beach out of sight of his wife and whispered secret words. By the power of his eloquence he lifted the kelp, the seaweed, the bladder-wrack into a curling cloud over the sea.

The cloud coiled and twisted. A sailing ship formed from the writhing blur. Gwydion spoke more words. His shape flickered . . .

In the glass castle, servants went to Arianrhod. 'My lady, two travellers have arrived in a wonderful ship. They say that if you will go ashore, they will make you shoes worthy of your fine feet.'

Arianrhod went ashore to find that the shoemakers were father and son.

As the father measured her foot, a wren flew overhead. Swift as thought, the son threw a needle. It struck the bird between sinew and bone.

Arianrhod laughed in admiration. She threw a coin at the lad. 'This is for the fair-haired boy with the skilful hand.'

'You have given him a name: Lleu Llaw Gyffes!' Which means the Fair-haired Boy with the Skilful Hand.

In a moment the ship became seaweed and the two shoemakers became her husband and son. She said, 'He may have a name, but I swear this fate upon him. He will have no weapons until I give them to him.'

Gwydion and Lleu waited a month. With every passing day Lleu became stronger and more skilful. Gwydion spoke secret words, so that their forms flickered . . .

In the glass castle, a servant went to Arianrhod. 'My lady, two storytellers are here. They say if you will admit them they will tell tales twisted with truth and trickery.'

In those days storytellers were always welcome, so they were admitted. She saw they were father and son . . .

The older storyteller told a tale of an invasion, a tremendous fleet of ships darkening the horizon. Such was the power of his eloquence that those who listened saw the pictures he painted with his words. The storyteller's voice became the shouts of warriors. The castle was under attack! Arianrhod and her servants armed themselves. She pressed weapons into the hands of the storytellers . . . in that instant the shouting stopped. The ships vanished. The storytellers became Gwydion and Lleu.

'He may have weapons,' she said, 'but I swear this fate upon him. He will not marry a woman born of any family on the Earth.'

Gwydion said, 'He will have a wife, mark my words.'

He took his son to the forest and spelled him a wife. They gathered flowers of white and red and gold. Gwydion whispered wizard's words. The flowers lifted and twisted in a spinning column . . .

The white petals became her skin,

  the gold her hair,

    the red her lips.

She was as beautiful as a spring morning. Lleu loved her at once. Gwydion named her Blodeuwedd, which means Face of Flowers. Blodeuwedd was a woman, but a woman newly born. She knew nothing of day and night, of love and hate, of truth and lies or right and wrong. She did not know how to speak, or eat, or walk. Everything was strange and new to her.

Gwydion gave his son a fortress and land and servants.

Little by little, Lleu taught his wife how to be human.

One evening Lleu went to visit his father. Blodeuwedd heard the sound of a hunting horn.

She ascended the walls of the fortress. She saw a nobleman pursuing a stag. His hounds caught it and brought it down. The nobleman drew his sword and killed the beast.

As she watched, Blodeuwedd felt a strange sensation. Her white cheeks went as red as her lips. She said to a servant, 'Go to him. Invite him to dine with me.'

'But, my lady,' said the servant, 'your husband is away. It is not right for you to be alone with this man.'

'My husband has taught me if a nobleman is travelling nearby at night he should be given food and shelter.'

Gronw, the nobleman, accepted the invitation. The moment he saw Blodeuwedd he was captivated by her beauty. All other sights, sounds, smells faded away. It was all he could do to stop himself from seizing her and kissing her in front of her servants.

That night a feast was held in Gronw's honour. It seemed to the servants that he and Blodeuwedd chatted politely. Had they been near enough to hear the words spoken, they would have been horrified.

Blodeuwedd whispered, 'Every day my husband tells me he loves me. I didn't know what he meant until now. Now I understand what love is. Because I love you.'

'There is no part of me that does not love you.'

'It isn't fair! Why did I fall in love with you and not my husband?'

'The heart goes where the heart wants.'

'How can I live with a husband I do not love?'

'There is a solution.'

'Tell me!'

'Kill him.'

'How? His father is a magician. Spells protect him.'

'There is always a way: a secret way. Your husband will know his own weakness. He trusts you. He loves you. He will tell you.'

When Lleu returned, he found his wife silent, distant. When they were alone together he said, 'What is the matter?'

Blodeuwedd told her first lie. 'Today I learned about death. How can I risk loving you when you can be snatched from me forever? Every mouthful of meat could choke you! Every time you ride your horse you could fall . . . you might leave me at any moment! This is torture.'

Lleu put his arms around his wife. 'Do not worry. My father has ensured it is hard for me to die. There is only one way.'

'Tell me how! Until I know, I cannot rest.'

'No normal weapon can harm me. I can only be killed with a spear that has been made during a year of Sundays.'

'But if an enemy heard these words, he could make such a spear!'

'Ah, but there is more. I cannot be killed indoors or outdoors, on horseback or on foot.'

She embraced him. 'This is impossible!'

'No, it is possible,' Lleu said, and he chanted:

'If I were to be struck with the spear
while standing with one foot on a goat's back
and one foot on the side of a bath,
half under a roof,
then I could be killed.'

She laughed and kissed him. 'That will never be!' And she sent word to Gronw.

For a year of Sundays he made the spear.

When he sent word the spear was finished, she pretended to be unhappy again. Of course, Lleu asked her why she was so distracted.

She said, 'I have been thinking again about how you could be killed. I am trying to remember all the things you mustn't do – there are so many! If you were to show me, then I would remember forever, and never again worry about your death.'

He laughed. 'If it would give you peace of mind . . .' And he ordered his servants to prepare a bath and fetch a goat.

The bath was placed half under the eaves of a roof. Lleu put one foot on the goat's back and the other one on the edge of the bath. He stretched out his arms to balance himself. 'If I were to be struck with the spear of Sundays now, then I could be killed.'

Gronw had been hiding nearby in a tree. His throw was sure and straight. The spear struck Lleu between the shoulder blades. Lleu gave a shrill scream. There was a fierce flash of light. His outstretched arms became wings. He became an eagle and rose into the sky, shrieking, the spear still stuck into his back.

Far away, Gwydion, riding, shuddered. He turned his horse. He rode for Lleu's hall. He disguised himself as a traveller. He found Gronw and Blodeuwedd feasting in the hall as lord and lady. It was as if Lleu had never existed.

Gwydion set off, searching for his son. Wherever he went he asked the same question: 'What curious things have happened here?'

One day he met a farmer who said, 'Each morning, when we release the pigs from their pen, our sow leaves the others behind and heads off into the next valley.'

Next morning, when the pigs were released, Gwydion followed the sow. Sure enough, she ran away from the herd, over the brow of a hill. Down into a valley she went, then up the other side. On that ridge there was a tree. One side of the tree was on fire from roots to crown. The flames were red and orange, blue and yellow. The other half of the tree was bright with green leaves. Amongst the leafy branches Gwydion saw an eagle. A spear was stuck in its back. It shrieked and shook its wings.

Lumps of rotting flesh fell. The sow eagerly devoured the flesh from the foot of the tree.

Gwydion chanted:

> 'A life of death.
> A tree of flames.
> A woman of flowers.
> A man of feathers.'

The eagle flew to his hand.

Gwydion drew out the spear. The eagle became Lleu again, but he was a pitiful thing, all skin and bone.

Gwydion took him to his castle. There Lleu lay until he was strong enough to stand.

He stood until he was strong enough to walk.

He walked until he was strong enough to run.

He ran until he was strong enough to ride.

Then Gwydion mustered an army and he and Lleu set off for revenge.

The guards on the walls of Blodeuwedd's fortress saw the army approaching. Blodeuwedd and Gronw fled, she one way, he the other.

Lleu pursued Gronw.

Gronw's horse stumbled and fell.

Lleu took Gronw to the place where he had lain in wait for Lleu.

'This,' said Lleu, 'is where you threw the spear. And this is the spear you threw at me. Now I will do the same.'

Gronw said, 'I know how it feels to take a life. I know the pain of remorse that will haunt you in the grey hours of the early morning. I beg you: don't wound yourself as I did. Show me mercy.'

He cast about. 'You see that stone? Let me use it as a shield.'

'I will show you more mercy than you showed me. Take it.'

So Gronw picked up the piece of slate and held it between him and Lleu.

Lleu drew back his arm and threw. The spear shattered the slate and pierced Gronw's body to the backbone.

Gwydion hunted down Blodeuwedd. When he captured her, he took her to the flaming tree.

She said, 'You are the closest I have to a father. You made me, and gave me to Lleu. Was it my fault that my heart went to another? I beg you, let me live.'

Gwydion chanted:

> 'A life of death.
> A tree of flames.
> A woman of flowers.
> A woman of feathers.'

Blodeuwedd's nose became a beak.

Her arms became wings.

Her feet became claws.

She became an owl. She flew into the leafy branches of the tree.

Ever since then, all other birds have hated and feared the owl.

A Word from the Author

These stories are very old. They are so old we don't know when they began. The earliest written version of any of them is more than 600 years old, but they were told by storytellers for hundreds of years before they were put on paper.

It is likely that these stories borrowed from other ancient stories and traditions. Some characters and ideas seem to come from Roman mythology, some from Celtic mythology, and some from medieval Christianity.

Other versions of these tales existed that were never written down, and so they have been forgotten. There were definitely other stories about these characters, stories that have been lost but which are referred to in other places. For example, some people think Pryderi became a great hero who had adventures of his own.

The stories that are left are incomplete. They are fragments of an elaborate pattern. Everyone who told these tales has done so for their own reasons, altering them to suit the tastes of the time. Just as when we turn a kaleidoscope, the fragments can be changed to make a different pattern.

This is what I have done. The lives we lead now are very different to the lives led by our ancestors long ago. Readers and listeners want a story that will charm and chill and thrill them. It doesn't matter whether it is based on fact or if it's thousands of years old. What matters most is whether the story can cast a spell over us.

These stories still cast a spell over me.

Would you have climbed the hill at Arberth? Would the hope of receiving a blessing be more important to you than the fear of receiving a curse? Would you bring the dead back to life? You would gain power, but at what cost?

The Wales in this book is a place of beauty and mystery. The stories help me see that beauty and feel that mystery as I travel through Wales today. When I go to Harlech or Narberth I imagine Brân sitting on the cliffs, or Pwyll hunting in the forest . . . I hope you will too.

Pronunciation Guide

These are stories which have been told and retold for many hundreds of years. To tell them in the Welsh way here's a rough guide to pronouncing some of the names. It uses common English words and syllables to help you. Put the stress on the elements in bold.

The First Branch

Dyfed (say 'dove' and then 'ed': **Dove**-ed)

Pwyll (say 'poi' like the start of 'point'. Now get ready to say the l at the start of 'lad', keep your tongue on the roof of your mouth, and hiss. Say Poi-lth)

Annwn (say '**Ann**-oon')

Arawn (say 'around' without the 'd' at the end: **A**-roun)

Hafgan (say '**Have**-gan')

Gwawl (rhymes with 'growl')

Teyrnon (say '**Tyre**-non')

Pryderi (say 'Prid-**airy**')

The Second Branch

Brân (rhymes with 'barn')

Nisien (say '**Niss**-yen')

Efnisien (say 'Ev-**niss**-yen')

Matholwch (say 'Math-**ol**-oo-ch' – the final sound is like the end of 'Ba**ch**')

Gwern (rhymes with 'bairn')

The Third Branch
Arberth (say '**Arr**-bairth')

The Fourth Branch
Gwydion (say '**Gwid**-yon')
Arianrhod (say 'Arry-**ann**-rode')
Caer (rhymes with 'tyre')
Dathyl (say '**Dath**-ill')
Dylan Eil Ton (say '**Dull**-ann **Isle** Ton': 'Ton' rhymes with 'Don')
Lleu (get ready to say the l at the start of 'lad', keep your tongue on the roof of your mouth and hiss. Now add 'eye')
Llaw (get ready to say the l at the start of 'lad', keep your tongue on the roof of your mouth and hiss. Now add 'ow' to rhyme with 'cow')
Gyffes (say **Guff**-ess)
Lleu Llaw Gyffes (put the three names together)
Blodeuwedd (Blod-**eye**-weth: the last part sounds like 'weth' in 'wether')
Gronw (say '**Gron**-oo')

Also by Daniel Morden:

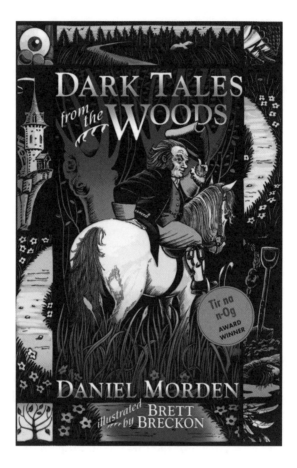

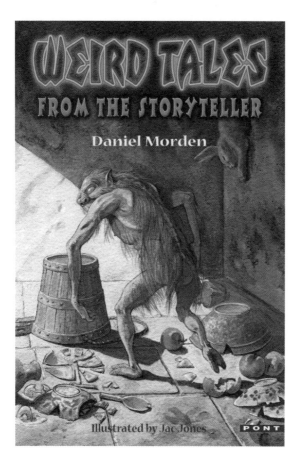

WEIRD TALES
FROM THE STORYTELLER

Daniel Morden

Illustrated by Jac Jones

PONT